REFLECTION

BY LIZY J CAMPBELL

Published by The Elite Lizzard Publishing Company

I dedicate this book to my nana, Margaret Blum, in heaven. I love you and miss you every day.

PROLOGUE

'Nothing could really prepare me for this life. I read all the Wizard of Oz books, Narnia, and The Never-ending Story. But this, this was something out of a science fiction novel, and somehow I was in it.

It's funny, I used to dive into those books like Bastian, trying to escape my reality. I felt like I was in those worlds, slipping through wardrobes into far-off places. Those books were my escape from my broken, abusive family. Now, I sit in my 200-foot glass dome on this forsaken alien planet that I am forced to call home. I wish for some sense of normalcy.

I long to go back. I take it all back what I said. The apparent anomalies of this pink-stained planet, with its deceptive beauty. What I once thought a wonder when I first arrived, is now a curse. We are all trapped here, thanks to 'her.'

CHAPTER 1

I woke from my bed by the alarm integrated throughout my room, the violent quakes shaking my glass dome.

As usual, the synthetic book I had been reading fell on a simulated hardwood floor, and with a muffled dull thud, evaporated. That used to startle me when I first came here six months ago, it doesn't anymore. Now, it's my only comfort and daily reoccurrence I can count on since I got here.

The quakes on this planet have become more frequent and are very troubling to me, since I have no idea what is causing it. I really need to find a way off this planet. I miss my home and earth. Well, if a park bench was a home.

I don't even know how these aliens knew I liked to read but; I do think it helps to keep me sane. Such a weird oddity that they would care for my wellbeing after abducting me.

The book, the one I used to read as a child, The Marvelous Land of Oz, started showing up three months ago. I, at least, take comfort in the old pleasures of home; even if they are simulated for my benefit.

Perhaps they are trying not to provoke violence in their guests. Who knows, I am just glad to have something familiar.

Thousands of glass pods are all lined up and are within the perimeters of the city as I look out. The pink hues of the sky are reflecting like a kaleidoscope over the glass pods. This makes it hard to stare at any one thing, due to how bright it is.

Its crystal white walls and pink clouds that surround it, are all tucked around the cylinder of the cathedral's transient walls with no roof. It looks like something celestial, a protective wall. Made from the mythology god,

Zeus? It really isn't though, but my mind wonders about to some attachable pleasantries, a way to try to connect myself to something from home.

The delicate veins in the walls look stained and blurry; they are incased throughout the structure. It has a glowing pink pulse, which rapidly blinks. It feels as though it is siphoning out or taking in, an unknown energy; making it feel alive.

Perhaps a great beast has swallowed me. I can feel it somehow, as I touch the surfaces of it in my room, it breathes.

I flick the button that hovers, although, it's not touching any surface. The glass dome proceeds to fog. It's set on a timer, so I must try to hurry to change into my uniform.

They are always watching.

It's not like I have a great variety of clothing to choose from. Only one pair of off duty clothing is provided to every person on this planet, by hieroglyphics.

I have deduced this on my own while being here. I laugh at the thought of it, I don't even know what fucking number I am. *If it even was a number.*

I seldom get to talk to anyone here, except for another humanoid who's in her first stages of transformation, named Ziv.

I think she used to be like me, until she was put in the box. She doesn't remember much, but she at least listens to my endless complaints with thoughtful blank expressions. She is more like a soundboard than an active participant in what it truly means to be a friend. I feel like they have erased her emotions along with a lot of the human likenesses that make us, well; us.

I have to find a way off this planet. I must get out of here; my mind keeps going back to that, and it's on repeat. This is my main objective; I want to go home. But I fear the only way in which I can, is if I can somehow, get close enough to kill their leader. *If you even CAN kill her.*

She sees us whenever she chooses by a series of capsule-like pod vessels that resemble a flower-like human eye and are attached to these types of guards or henchmen, as I like to call them.

When a human gets chosen for transformation, I would describe it as being put into glass pillboxes; but, slightly less rounded in shape. They barely fit the average sized human.

I am five feet, ten inches tall; I am one of the tallest species of humans left here. Not that I have seen any actual humans, only these variations of transformed ones and for some reason are shorter than me. I am also the only one of the ones they haven't put in those boxes. *Yet.*

I haven't been reprogrammed while in hyper sleep.

I think there might be something wrong with me.

My hair is jet black to the middle of my back, and I have a voluptuous yet fit figure, as us earthlings would say back in 2014. I still need to wear these old prescription glasses too as I am blind as a bat. Last year, I was back on my planet, sleeping on a park bench and homeless and 18, before they took me against my will.

But enough about me, I am working on giving information about earth to an alien central data program, which feels a lot like a sonogram we had back on earth. That's what is keeping me alive, so much as I can tell. So, if I can keep bullshitting my way around here, I should be ok, *maybe*.

My name is Unum, and on earth, I was nothing more than a waste of space.

But here, here I am valued.

Well, I would like to think I am.

CHAPTER 2

I cover my head over my pillow, my parents are so loud and obscene. They don't care that I'm in the room beside them with these paper-thin walls. What else is new, either they are in love, or someone is bleeding or bruised.

There is no in-between.

Well, that is to say, when my mom and my stepdad are actually together, that is. They can't stay together for more than a year a time. They have a huge fight and breakup; she proceeds to throw his stuff over the balcony. Including any new things that were meant for us. TV, the Nintendo game system,... you name it. It's all gone if he's the one who paid for it. '*Can't have reminders,*' she would say.

He's a drug addict, drunk, and my mom likes to drink a lot too. A great combination for a family. But at least I had my nan who took me away from it, as much as she could. She saved me from them, I miss her. Since her death I felt as though I lost a mother. She took care of me and loved me better than my own mom.

My dad's hammer hurled into my door which startled and frightened me. It made a huge smashing noise, that even my dog's tail went between his legs. He decided to hide, in an attempt to crawl under my bed. Poor Sammy, he was a sensitive black Labrador not yet a year old. Another great idea of my moms, who never kept pets for more than six or seven months, due to allergies.

I launched myself into the closet for protection.

Sammy followed suit. I loved my closet, it was the only place I felt safe, ever. I had my books, my pencils and paper and my favorite toys. My little ponies, barbies. I used to braid their hair and take them on blanket mountain adventures on my bed when I was younger. They were my only friends besides the furry friends who briefly stayed with us.

Ken, barbies' husband, never did anything but sleep or sit on a recliner, much the same as my stepdad.

I didn't care for that doll at all, his hair was molded plastic to his head. To fake in my mind. At least have synthetic hair like barbie.

Anyway, the only time I really got to know my mom was when they broke up, for a short while. I got to spend real time with her, it was peaceful and quiet.

I loved it, but I knew my mom didn't. She would always cry every night for him, I could hear her in the bedroom next to mine. She couldn't live without a man. I always wondered why I wasn't enough for her, to be protected, to be loved.

***

CHAPTER 3

The henchmen, as I liked to call them, were on the war path this morning; the flashing red strip of light along the walls always meant something bad was happening. I had no idea what to do or how to communicate with these species; which just caused me to panic.

We were all segregated here, as far as I could tell, each to a post. I never saw any of the others together in one place.

I am sure there are others like me, I see the pods. There was Ziv.

Ziv, is first generation in transformation into one of them.

The henchmen were a massive contrast to the neon and pastel pinks on this planet. All black coverings and if they had any skin, it was carefully covered.

I'd never seen it.

The fabric looked as though it was made from some kind dull, black matted material. The style put me in mind of gothic steampunk in a matrix movie. The jacket went from high around the top of their heads to the floor. It had a series of eyes instead of buttons throughout the outfit.

Watching from all angles.

They are the enforcement and protection should things go south, the nightspect's.

"Hey, what's happening? Why is the program flashing like that?" I ran over to my screen since I realized I had zoned out.

The second-generation synthetic humanoid robot turned in my direction with its brass-colored metallic neck. Clearly, I had thought the robot would ignore me... like it always had.

He hovered over and his hand, in a flash, grabbed my neck and began to squeeze. His face had no emotions, and his eyes were lifeless, just yellow, and glowing.

“I ... I am sorry..” I tried to speak, gagging on my spit, as my limited air supply was being cut off.

Lifted up by only my neck, the android threw me to the floor. I stayed there frozen. A technique I learned as a child. My whole body shook. This was the first time I had encountered anyone here so closely.

Petrified.

Urine began to trickle down my pants. Could it read my thoughts? I pondered this as I put my head down and Ziv did not dare move a muscle toward helping the situation.

This cacotopia of hell I was living in, was starting to bewilder me and work my last frazzled nerve.

Ziv continued to work, and briefly looked in my direction with what looked like synthetic sympathy.

This android spoke, or at least I think that’s what it was, for the first time since being on this planet, and for a minute; I thought my ears would bleed. The tone in which it spoke was unlike any sound I had ever heard before. It reverberated off the inner confines of my brain and created a dull pain in my cerebellum. For the first time in my life, I knew exactly where it was.

I can no longer speak or control my muscle movements; my body begins to vibrate. I'm foaming at the mouth; I can only hold my head and scream, before passing out.

***

CHAPTER 4

The kids at school are just as bad as my parents.

They are always just a little bit too enthusiastic about squad crowding me in the playground. Teasing me about the hand-me-down clothes, and my glasses that never suited my thin face.

I was tall for eleven, and gangly for my age. My parents were religious, an added bonus to my plight.

They didn't want me to participate in any activities that might not be in accordance with the views of the sacred sanctimony of a lie they called, a religion. This only added to the bullying. They had made sure that I would be isolated from everyone here, in these cemented halls of hell, that was the public education system.

I remember attempting to go home one evening, when a larger brute decided to skate off and up the back of my leg and onto my lower back; as I fell to the concrete like a ragdoll. The laughter still echoes in the halls of my skull to this day.

I had to reevaluate my claims of mortality, since I was taught as much. The bruises I sustained from my parents, and then these sadistic children; I truly begged to differ for some miracle to befall me, to get me out of this place.

It would be years of this abuse, junior kindergarten until grade six. I finally thought I had escaped when I changed schools. It was undoubtedly not the end for me.

Did it toughen me up? No, it broke me over and over, and over again. Until a thick scab of callus formed over the wounds inflicted from of both my parents, and my peers.

I became numb to it, my mind protecting me.

All I had were my books. Words, dreams, and those brief moments with my nan. That gave me time to heal and find some sense of self happiness. Every night, since I arrived here on this pink planet, I have been reliving my childhood through my dreams no, rather, my nightmares.

I don't understand it, but I wish it would end.

***

CHAPTER 5

I woke up on a medical table with a pair of pink neon ring eyes staring back at me. The centers were black as coal. I had never seen an alien so beautiful as this.

It must be the final generation transformation into the species, I thought to myself. Its slender smooth skin and perfected lips. It looked like I imagine an alien should. It was beautiful, but cold.

It hovered over to me with an instrument in its slender hands. Tiny lights that were blinking from the machine reflected on its slightly shiny skin, as she held it above my forehead.

"How are you feeling?" it said.

I watched those perfect lips that didn't move.

Am I dreaming?

“I am a little sore in my neck still. Can you understand me? Do you speak my language?' I spoke to it, out loud.

It was staring at me as though it was cutting through my soul, like laser beams. It never blinked, not even once.

“I am speaking to you through telekinesis, I do not wish to injure you like that other exon android did. He was trying to warn you to stay out of his way, unfortunately, he is flawed.” It hovered across the floor to grab another piece of equipment.

I looked around the room. The place had white crisp walls but with flecks of glittery crystalized neon pinks and violets reflecting in it. It looked and resembled some kind of granite. It made me laugh. The irony of finding human-like products in an alien world.

"Why is it I can understand you now?"

To the left of me was a table of some liquid metal, that looked as though it was in constant motion; and yet it stayed in one place. The table held other peculiar tools that this alien needed.

The room was clean and bare otherwise. It felt sterile. I imagine that I must be the hospital, or infirmary.

"I have inserted a chip into your ear to translate our language." It said.

I watched it, observing and taking everything in. The outfit it wore was like its pinkish skin. One bright pink eye on the center of her back, and one smaller on the front where a label of her name and rank would be if it was a doctor on earth. It was similar to the eyes on my uniform and hat they made me wear, but the color was different.

Those organic eyes were sprinkled throughout the confinement of this white prison, I called home.

I smirked to myself and tried to ignore the mounding pressure of wanting to run out of the room, screaming like a madwoman.

They were always watching, *ugh*...

"I see." I put my pinky into my ear and felt nothing.

Taking in the view, I pushed my unpleasant thoughts of having an alien chip in my head. Great, what else have they done to me while I was out.

I could see outside for the first time since I have been on this planet.

Without thinking, I got off the table and walked over to the view. “WOW.” I said, I had never seen it from this side before.

It was all a pink glow of serenity. It was stunning. It didn’t seem real.

Puffy pink clouds lined the skies, and as I looked out and below, a bright pink path intertwined and weaved in and out of tropical forests and flowers. It practically dissolved into the landscape. At the other end of the field, much further away; it seemed vastly darker in comparison.

The trees here looked more like mounds of alien planet matter; there were no leaves, like on earth. The green contrasts-streaked vast landscapes in places. Those, tree trunk like things, protruded out of the ground in various sizes and shapes. They were not as colorful as the tints of bright neon fuchsia pink flowers that dotted the landscape.

It hovered over to where I was standing and observed the view with me, from the half circle glass dome window.

"Ah, so that's what you perceive. They are what you call flowers called; inflorescent roseus. These angiosperms produce the color you call the color, fuchsia pink. It is a distinction on our planet. They are vital, they are life. They hold great power."

I wanted to question the alien more, but it took me by the arm and escorted me out of that room and into my glass dome, through a series of glass tubular tunnels.

On the way, I looked about the vastness of this place.

It felt like we were in a series of neuron stems. I could look above me and see others like the alien beside me. Only it showed and for the first time, I saw many others in distinct alternative stages of transformation, walking through the tunnels in different directions.

I could no longer see the outside; we were within the confines of the inner white walls I had become familiar and accustomed. I continued to look up, past the floors, and I could see those powder pink clouds of outside and the transition to the stars above.

My door evaporated as I approached, I was home. It escorted me inside and checked my forehead once more. The lights on the machine formed a line straight across, this time it didn't flash.

It removed it from me and put it away. It had dissolved into its outfit like there might have been a pocket, the apparatus simply absorbed revealing nothing, or any lump as to where it was.

“You are well now, human. You may have many dreams tonight."

"Great… Hey, do you have a name? I would like to know the name of my nurse," I chuckled.

“I am afraid human; you would not be able to pronounce it. Since 'nurse,' is your idea of a name for me, you may call me that. Nurse."

"Um, well that's not a name, it's a title given for what it is that you do. Never mind." I was feeling hungry suddenly and needed to eat my two magic alien cakes. It came from the drawer that appeared and materialized by pressing a series of buttons, near my hovering bed.

"You may call me, Altha."

It turned and the door evaporated once more. As it slid out, the larger eye blinked on its back.

"Altha,"... I mimicked, I supposed she is a female then.

I ate with feverish hunger.

***

CHAPTER 6

The only best friend I ever had in school was Robin.

She played with me every summer. All summer in fact, up until grade three. We did everything together. I used to watch her grandmother pick the dandelions out of the fields, right behind our building for her tea. I thought it was funny, no one else did this in the complex. I think that is what made her memorable, to me, anyway.

September was here, and it was the first day of grade four. I was excited to see Robin because this summer, I didn't spend much time at her house. It seemed like she was always busy; she barely answered the phone.

I saw her off in the distance, I waved wildly. "Robin, over here!" I yelled out, I was so excited to see her.

Robin didn't smile when she saw me, like she always did. Something was wrong, my heart sank even before she started to walk over to me.

"Hi, so… I don't really want to be friends anymore. I thought that you would have got the hint over the summer. I didn't want to hurt your feelings but, your weird and my parents don't want me hanging out with you anymore… ok? Bye." Robin turned and walked away, back to her new group of friends.

That was it. My heart shattered and broke into a million pieces.

My home life was hard enough, now I didn't even have a friend.

Latoya, b-lined over to me, "Hey, you look sad. Robin not wanting to be a loser's friend anymore? You should have known this was coming, right? Look at you and look at her. Where did you get those clothes from, Goodwill? The Bargain shops? You share your clothes with your grandma? Wow, such a nice skirt, grandma." Everyone around me started to laugh. Another girl in her group said it was probably from a dumpster. They all laughed even louder.

I couldn't hold in the tears, they just kept streaming down my face as she continued to berate me.

That was me, that was my life. Constant bullying at school, and constant abuse at home.

I just stood there frozen, not uttering a word.

I waited until her boredom of making fun of me had set in, then she walked away with her usual nose in the air and the crowd of followers were close behind. The popular kids.

I just kept crying silently, until the bell rang.

I picked up my backpack I had from last year, that was sitting on the ground, hidden under my 'granny' skirt. I death gripped it like it was a life raft and begrudgingly walked inside.

The sweat poured down my face, as I jerked my body up in bed. It was still dark.

A nightmare again of my past, and this one made me wide awake.

This meant I would have to try to go to sleep again, until the alarm went off.

I dreaded it.

I knew I had to get plenty of rest to keep my wits about me. I laid my head down and flipped the sweaty pillow over to the cool side, and once more, I wished myself to dream something different.

It made no difference; I tossed and turned the rest of the night.

***

CHAPTER 7

The pink field of flowers were vast and untouched by human, or alien hands. Not even the first and second generations at least. I learned a few things. Now that I had this new chip installed, it fed me information about how this planet operated.

I often tried to catch a glimpse of what outside looked like. No one was allowed to go near the flowers, only the hybrid humanoids or organic androids, for lack of a better term.

As they emerged from the pillbox cubicle houses, they set off to work. Incubated for the equivalent of ten earthly year increments. They were programmed to take care and find new ways to use the thermorganictech in order to advance the race, and to further perfect the species. As far as I could tell anyway.

'Her' as they called the master, and creator of this planet, had carefully selected humans on earth to be brought here, twenty light years from earth. Bearing in mind the vastness of that expanse from earth to mars is a mere five light years.

Way out here, there was no escape for humans, except through the channels of alien technology.

Unmanned drones were sent every year to gather more humans up, until they brought me.

Some of them while being transported, died during the journey, and needed to be replaced.

Only the tough-minded ones made it here and

made it past the second term transformation. Which was another ten-year incubation, and what we humans perceived in earthly years, was done quicker in terms of the advanced alien tech. The total process of transformation from human to alien species would take thirty human years.

The process is an Infusion and interlaced with organic matter, that is constantly and slowly, streaming into the bloodstream, and oxygenating organic matter into the human lung to help it be able to breathe on this planet's atmosphere. It was a slow and precise process. It had taken years to create and perfect the balance. Each was inspected weekly for progress.

Most of who that made it past the first five years were unlikely to die, but there were still odd cases. And it left the remaining humans, in smaller numbers every year.

I often wondered what they did with the bodies, as I never saw it. But from gathering and deducing information, I have learned a lot.

Once the third generation were let out, they were immortal. No longer in need of oxygen and food, like other organisms needed. One injection of that organic planet matter and it would regulate them and their new bodies for a year at a time.

I couldn't imagine not having the joy of eating my favorite foods. Other than the fact that those cakes I ate were sweet they had no flavor. I longed for a plate of spaghetti smothered in cheese. Hopefully, they can gather that data and upgrade the food around here.

The thermorganictech, is the engineering and harnessing the organic alien plant matter, creating a heat source and viable resource for human injection. The species here that abducted me is called Imagorna, and they reflect their creator.

The organic matter is coursing with alien life in their bodies and the pinkish color is bright with third generation skin.

Being part of the organic alien plant matter, changed their skin, which is also pink.

It reminded me of how flamingos get there pink color in a way.

It makes me laugh if I simplified it, *'you eat too much pink, you become pink.'*

Anyway, the synthetic DNA in a human is altered and perfected to coexist as one with the planet, named Malaxate.

At least I knew where I was, not that it helped matters. I don't want to be changed into one of them.

***

CHAPTER 8

I walked to my assigned station, not very awake from last night's nightmares.

Ziv was already busy at work, doing whatever it was she was supposed to do. She never tells me anything. She doesn't object to my banter at least, so I have stopped trying to get information out of her; besides, she's like talking to a brick wall.

Now that I have a chip in my ear, I have a better understanding of what the objective of this planet is. They want the same thing I do; they want to leave. That gives me little comfort. I hated life on earth but now, I would give anything to see it again.

"Hey Ziv, I see your already hard at it." I elbow her gently, trying to initiate a conversation.

Ziv looks intently at me, "Yes, I am indeed. Please go to your station and begin your work."

My mouth dropped.

That was the first two sentences I ever heard Ziv say besides, hi and bye.

"She speaks! Well, you can say more than two things. It's nice to hear your voice." I smile at her.

"Please, go to your station and begin your work." Ziv says robotically and repeatedly, attempting to smile at me, which is creepy.

"Okay, okay. Your language is limited... I get it." I blurt out as I walked back to my area.

The android male is watching me I pick up from the corner of my vision, a shiver goes down my spine. I turn away fast, hoping he hasn't noticed me, as I was just looking in his direction, just moments before.

I feel a hot hand on my shoulder... I stop, frozen. My body begins to vibrate from the memories of what he did to me, I know it's him again.

"My apologies, human, for scaring you as I did. That was not very polite, I am told. It will not happen again now that Altha has inserted that chip in your ear and are able to understand our language."

I turn my head to face him, he is standing too close to me. "No problem." I verbalize without making an audible sound.

"Altha tells me you like names. My name is Torga. You may refer to me as this when you need to address me...Unum." Torga turns, leaving. It does not wait for my reply and goes back to work.

I look in the direction of Ziv and she glances at me, almost knowing I was going to look at her. *Weird sixth sense, perhaps.*

Torga, is made of a dull metalized material, yellow beady eyes incased in tunnel pair of glass. Half of his body is structured like a robot. The lower half has wheels in replacement of legs. He is vastly less attractive, and the metals composition is a brown. A crust is forming in the joints of his entire body. Weird though, as he hovered like Altha, I guess an upgrade.

He is an experiment that was never replicated.

Lunch is different this time, I have permission to join Ziv and Torga. At first, I am not sure of where they are taking me.

Down to a large area I have never been, it is filled with floating tables and pod-like chairs. There is other first and second-generation humans and Imagorna species, all scattered throughout the room.

As I walk by, I hear everything, and I can understand the conversations they are having. What they are working on, what they are laughing about. It almost feels normal, like it would be on earth in a workroom lunchroom.

I laugh hysterically at my odd coworkers, and Ziv raises an eyebrow at me in bewilderment. I am ignored for the most part as I go to sit at one of the tables, I am nothing they haven't seen before I guess.

"What? This is the best lunch since I have been on this godforsaken planet, Ziv! I learned so much today." Ziv, she only ate once a week since her first incubation, I discover. Today, she was chewing very slowly on her pink cakes. Mine were always a slightly different color, purple hues.

"Nice to see the human is feeling more like us, then an alien. Get it human? I made for you, a human joke." *I reflected on that.*

"Huh, yeah, I guess so. You need to work on your material, Ziv."

***

"Go to your room! I can't stand your face; you look just like your dad!"

My mom was infuriated with my stepfather, who left, for the millionth time. She was taking it out on me.

"You never want me to be happy, do you? It's you that causes us to break up all the time, you know that. You brat! I hate you; I wish I never had you."

I went into my room and cried.

I knew I didn't cause them to break up, but it hurt all the same.

"What did I do? I hate my face; my mom hates my face. I am worthless!" I was mad at me too.

I screamed into my pillow from the frustration of the emotional turmoil of the constant abuse. I never knew it was not okay, it was my life. I didn't know the difference.

All I knew was that I was never good enough for her, never good enough at school.

Not even when my nan told me I was beautiful.

I thought she was just trying to be nice to me. They all just pitied me. The somber realization that you were born to be a personal punching bag for everyone was a lot to carry for a thirteen-year-old.

I was going to church, even if my parents rarely showed up, I was made to.

I had to make up stories constantly as to why they were always absent. My most used excuse was that she had a cold and was sick. I could feel them not believing it.

One lady took me aside and said, "You don't have to lie to protect your parents, that is not something a little girl should have to be responsible for. I can see the stress in you every time someone asks you. I know child. You don't have to hide it from me."

I hugged her so tight and just cried.

Months of frustration just dripped into the fabric of her polyester jacket.

I wanted to scream.

I wanted so badly to tell them how my parents treated me. But my tongue stayed lodged in my throat. I couldn't and wouldn't betray them like they did me. I would not and did not tell a soul.

Today at school, I was wearing my corduroy pants in hot weather, waiting for the bruises to heal from my last beating.

The teacher stopped to ask me if I was hot.

I told her no with the sweat beads pouring down my bruised back. The belt buckle welts took longer to go down this time.

I couldn't wait to go home, so I could change and wear shorts in my room, at least.

I finally got home to my mother fuming again. "Why was the volume on the stereo so loud? I went to turn it on, and it blasted my ears! Did you touch it? You know you're not allowed to touch the stereo. Well, did you?"

"No." I stood my ground.

She has been relentless lately. I don't know what I did but lately, nothing I did or said was right and I am getting smacked for it. I was getting tired of her screaming at me. I lived here too and if I wanted to listen to some music and scream at the world while they were gone, to get my frustrations out, I should at least be allowed to.

"You're a liar! I hate liars!" She smacked me in the face and then kept on hitting me.

I backed into the hallway of our house near my bed-room, desperately trying to get away from her fists and slaps. She wasn't stopping this time. I covered my face with my arms and slid down the wall to protect what I could of my body. That's when she decided to start kicking me in the crotch. I was protecting my face with my hands as she grabbed a handful of my hair and proceeded to lift me up with it.

"Get up, and take your punishment, you liar! Just wait until your dad gets home, you want him to discipline you?"

I got up without thinking and slapped her in the face. I was now taller than my five-foot four-inch bulldog of a mother.

I had enough.

"How DARE you!"

She backed up from me, and her eyes for the first time in my life, afraid. *Afraid of me.*

I had seen that look when my stepdad broke her nose, cracked her skull, and perforated her ear drum. Now that look was for me.

I was not sorry.

For the lifetime of pain, bruises, and tears, I was not allowing her to use me as a punching bag, not anymore.

CHAPTER 10

The fields of the planets inflorescent roseus plants, contained in the center of the organism, was a living, breathing, alien being. So microscopic, it was impossible to see with the naked eye.

The center had its own planetary life system. This was connected by its roots that were interconnected underground, in a series of intricate and delicate mazes.

When stepping off the pink pathway, the ecosystem, being so delicate, would destroy vital pieces of its system. Just by pressure alone, if anything other than the weight of the native species went on it; caused immense damage.

The planet hangs in the balance, and it would temporarily cause a major catastrophic event. From quakes to the Imagorna structures, the production of the flowers itself is what kept the planet's core sustained.

As for the alien's beasts, they cannot be viewed easily at the celestial tower above. The species or animals if you will, are camouflaged by the scenery. But if you stood very still, you could see one.

They would be defined in populations as rats that hide in plain sight in overpopulated cities, like New York.

The native animals that sport these razor sharp teeth, also cut through human bone. Their size is comparable to that of an earthly baby rabbit and up to as large as a raccoon. It is as dangerous as a piranha if it's on the path to food.

Fruit from the roseus flower also yields food for the humans and aliens to sustain them. But more importantly, it is too slowly prep humans for their introduction to transformation.

A lesson first learned after the first batch of humans died in two the first trial weeks of incubation. They needed to be whined and introduced to organic matter, so as to not shock their system. Like any foreign organism being introduced in a transplant, the body needed to be accepting of it.

The Imagorna are always looking to please the humans. This was deemed essential for sustaining there health, as was learned through Unum.

They recognized the need for joy, to keep humans happy. Realizing they needed to keep them content, or they would fall ill and inevitably die off.

They discovered humans enjoyed cakes, the Imagorna now presented the food in much the same way to ensure it would be received well.

Unum, a valuable source of information, has made a great contribution to the race.

The aliens have also made the glass homes with plenty of light ensuring for a less stressful human, requiring a synthetic vitamin D. The pink sun in the sky was made to simulate an earthly one.

Using the tech inside the glass domes, intricate sensitive information was used to draw out vital information as they slept. Air pumped into the pods contained pure oxygen, another gift of the plants evolving abilities to provide adequately for human survival.

Each of the humans' dreams played an important part in knowing what soothed them, to create a more receptive response to the overall treatment.

Unum has taken the longest for the aliens to figure out. She has much distress, and for months the nightmares have been recorded. It has taken a while before finding a small glimpse of hope, she found joy in reading books.

'She' would allow such pleasures, as it was the benefit of the colony as a whole.

In time Unum, after much prepping and introduction to the thermorganictech food infused cakes, would hopefully be more receptive to the treatment and transition process down the line. *But time, they did not have.*

The master,' She,' was in an incredibly fragile state.

As everything on the planet was interconnected to each other, she was at a disadvantage. She needed to be able to become a separate entity to start this process. She needed the Imagorna to be self-sustainable and farm the land to lift the roots that bound her and them.

'After years of the transference of the planet and farming of its roseous, was it just beginning to become a separate entity?'

Altha finishes recording her thoughts and studies and sends them off to the central data for further investigation.

***

CHAPTER 11

I walked the through same white halls this morning as I had been for what felt like, years. My uniform untouched with age or dirt. I think I am now 20, but it's hard to tell, I have lost track of how long I have been here.

A sudden shift in the building threw me to the wall. "What the fuck was that?" rubbing my now banged up left side of my shoulder.

I looked and a hairline crack proceeded to creep up the wall and continue beyond the floors, ceiling, and hallways.

In the center of the building, it was open to view the other side of the spiral walkway incased in glass. If you looked with your face pressed against the glass, you could just barely see a sliver of outside between the walls. That pink was unmistakable.

Torga ran past me nearly crashing into me, with Ziv close behind.

"Hey, what's going on?" I called out, shifting out of the way.

I started to jog behind them to keep up, "where are you going?"

"There's been a shift on the planets system, you must go back to your room and wait instructions." Ziv called out. Torga didn't bother to look behind and robotically moved quicker than usual.

I stopped running and stood there as the others bumped into me and ran past me in a panic to wherever it was they were rushing to get to.

I never had reason to disobey, but now, this might be the opportunity I needed.

I waited for the last few of them to run by me before I followed. I was not turning around to go back to my room, I needed a ship or something. I would figure it out the rest on the way.

The hallway seemed to go on forever, I had never been in this area before. Nothing looked familiar, except those outside walls that never changed.

The alien granite wall had just changed sides all of a sudden, and a window appeared. It was now on the right side of me. I could see outside as I peeked out but couldn't see anything, as there was cloud covering everything.

Those fluffy, angelic pink clouds.

I kept going and followed the most direct tunnel.

The luminescent lights began to flicker above my head as I continued.

'Crack!'

Another shift threw me to the ground, this time there were a series of hairline cracks fanning out in all directions along the wall.

"Oh, shit!" I got up and moved away from the cracks.

No one came or went.

Silence.

A series of doors like my room were lined up down the hall and were not opening. I tried, but nothing. It could have been bed chambers for the others.

A bright pink ray shone in and bounced off the opposite wall. Another window. I started to jog over to it, now I would be able to see.

I looked out and again I was stopped by the cloud cover. *Dammit!*

I looked down the hall and saw something half pink half black flash by the corner of my vision.

"What the hell was that?"

My heart started beating faster, sweat began to form on my brow. I wonder if that was the leader. I turned to continue further, despite my growing fears.

A series of nightspects dressed in all black, suddenly formed a barrier and stood in my way. I backed up, and lifted my arms, I wanted to try to explain myself.

"Hi, yeah, I know I am supposed to be in my room, but I wanted to help. Can I help?"

The heat coming off of them was tremendous. My eyes stared to water.

They said nothing, but moved forward causing me to continue to walk backward from the burning heat they gave off.

"Hey, I don't want any trouble, okay?"

Faster than my eyes could see, one of them grabbed me and lifted me with its four arms and threw me violently against the wall.

The impact knocked me instantly unconscious.

Blood from my head spilled out onto the pristine white floor and pooled out, soaking my hair.

***

CHAPTER 12

I stuffed all that I could manage into two black garbage bags in my room. Everything of my life that I could take with me.

My cat, Bumkin, came over and rubbed my leg. I wanted so badly to take him with me, he was my only friend in the world; I loved him so much. I picked him up and cried into his beautiful grey, tabby stripped fur. He was the longest pet I ever had. He and I instantly bonded. I was the only one who took care of him, due to my mom having allergies and anxiety. I also took him to the vet; I did everything for him.

There I stood, frozen in time, looking about my bedroom as I felt him purring, vibrating loudly on my chest.

"I will come back for you as soon as I can find a place, I love you. Wait for me."

I hear the honk of the van outside and I grab my heavy bags. I can't take Bumkin with me because I don’t have a place of my own yet. But I will come back for him. I promised. But for now, it was time to get the hell out of this shitshow.

I open the door, and smack headfirst into my mom coming through the front door.

“Hi, there’s a guy here for you? says he’s here to pick you up? Are you working? That’s earlier than... what’s those bags for?”

“I am leaving mom, I am done.”

“NO, please, your dads gone now, you can't leave me too!”

I felt sorry for her, for a split second.

Tears started to form in my eyes, "I can’t mom. I gotta go.”

I don’t and can't look back as I throw my bags, all that’s left of my life, into the back of the van. I hop in and refuse to look up at her.

“Are you sure you want to do this? I mean, she can’t be all that bad, you know, I used to hate my mom too, but it does pass. How about you come to my place for a few hours, cool down, and see how you feel later okay?” The driver, Jay, says to me.

“Listen, I can’t okay, just get me out of here.” My voice cracks as I talk to Jay, and tears streaming down my face won’t let me look at him.

Instead, I keep my face turned to the passenger side window. I look out at what I hope to never see again, this neighborhood, or her. If it wasn’t for Bumkin, I never would.

The two months before I decided to leave was the last time my dad moved back home.

We had moved into a basement, and it was really a nice place, but the fights continued.

My stepdad was drinking, and my mom was continuing, well, to be my mom. Cutting out pages in the paper so he couldn't see it. Dubbing movies and erasing parts with any scenes with any other women she deemed as more attractive than her. She didn't want him looking at other women. She trying to control him and he hitting in retaliation instead of leaving for good.

I would watch him viewing the same movie repeatedly, Treasure Island or 20,000 leagues under the sea. I enjoyed the movie sometimes. I came to watch it with him, but only if the storm of my parents' arguments had cleared up.

I was wrong.

My dad had two beers in him, and the fighting began once more. I slipped into my sanctuary, my bedroom, and closed the door.

Not that it helped at all.

I could hear it escalating, the muffled elevated voices, then I heard him slap her, like so many times before.

But this time, I had enough.

He threw the glass beer bottle against our kitchen wall. The glass shattered and was dripping down the freshly painted wall, the stench of it triggering my anger.

I saw him with his fist in her face, telling her he was going to give her something to scream about, all I could see was red. I grabbed the knife from the dishrack and pointed it in his direction. I went between them and held it close to his neck.

"Get away from her!" I screamed.

"Oh, look, your daughters a tough guy, are you a tough guy, huh? Hmm?" He grabs my arm with the knife still in my hand and puts it under his neck. He pushes the tip of the blade into his skin.

"Do it, I dare you. Do it. Come on tough guy." He then pushes me into my mom, and I almost lose my balance. My mom proceeds to go after me.

"Don't you dare touch her!" My mom rips the knife from my hands, looks over at me and then slaps me in the face.

All I can think in this moment is, 'mom, you're fucked.'

My stepdad leans against the wall and wipes a hand across his thick black hair that's producing sweat from his forehead.

"Yeah, I'm done. Attacked in my own home. I will not live with you and your constant yelling any longer. I can't live like this anymore. Look at your daughter. What are we doing here? This is just so wrong." My stepdad takes a last look at my mom and a last look at me, before walking out the door.

“This is all your fault you know; you always hated him. You never wanted me to be happy. You were jealous. Just like you were when you were a little girl, and you are the same now.” My mom was yelling in my face.

I had no words.

The person who verbally abused me, beat me, and tormented me for my entire life, I had just tried to protect. She thinks I am responsible for the fucking joke her marriage is, and this new breakup too. I am beginning to see that if I don’t leave soon I will not be able to make it out alive.

***

CHAPTER 13

Altha stares at the screen from the highest location in the tower, as Unum's dreams come flooding in. She has only one interest, one objective, figure out what makes Unum tick.

The room is filled with monitors on everyone, all vital signs are kept under strict watch. From here, she can see the test subjects, check heart beats and the humans in the hubs that are undergoing the different stages of transformation.

The highly sophisticated technology, only brought about by combining thermorganictech and Pico technology.

This technology uses the manipulation of a heated organic fuel cell, which when combined in its purest form, creates learning macrobiotic machines. These can help the species formulate the perfect pico-tech cell. A learning macrobiotic machine that creates a host environment for the plant to continue to grow independently inside the human body. Thrive even, the added bonus is immortality to the species in return to the host.

It's so tiny, it bypasses the human's immune system which if seen would attack the foreign matter.

The accepting gases that are slowly seeped into the humans' pores, oxygen, and bloodstream, to begin the slow process of change and acceptance.

Because humans are consistently being infused with this organic matter over a long period of time, under hyper sleep, the body will choose to accept and receive all the nutrients needed to sustain them. The body has no choice.

This is forcing the human body to decide to embrace the offerings given, in order to survive. Human nature is to evolve rather than die. Something the Imagorna have witnessed in the beginning test phases and have utilized.

Since the leader's arrival, the species of the Imagorna have slowly been infusing the planets resources into the chosen humans.

To make not only a superior perfected race of immortality, but more importantly, in the hopes of separating them from the attachment of the planet.

With enough of the species having the living plant matter within them, they will not be devoid of the precious life-giving alien plant life. So, they will be able to leave now because they are the planet itself but now in smaller quantities. The extinction will never happen now, and life will live on in many, instead of one planet.

Only with Unum, everything that had worked for the others has had no effect on her.

They continue to monitor her dreams in order to better understand, and to find something to use in order to gain insight as to why nothing is working.

So far, all they know is that she has been abused and bullied all her life. She has built an internal resistance to influences around her and she defies the normal human threshold for emotional physical pain sustained, in her life. She has become an anomaly.

The alien race that used to play among the stars, is now resorting to abduction in order to save the species. They used to bounce from one planet to another, free to come and go as they wished, explorers.

They are prisoners of their home planet.

The race is unsure of how it all began, or even when they discovered 'her,' to be the leader over them.

The last of the humans were shipped out by drone, and it is imperative that Unum begin to be assimilated, like the others.

The alien's memory of how or what they were before, has somehow been erased.

'Her,' refuses to divulge that information to them.

Altha pushes the button for Unum to come out of her comma, as she's awoken, it is time for her to change into her uniform.

It's been 6 weeks since Unum's head trauma with the nightspects.

Altha, spent most of the time creating an organicthermopictech cranial head cover to heal the wound.

Her body yet again rejected it, making Unum's healing process slow. Yet the brain activities show that the nightmares are still steadily continuing to go through a timeline since she's landed.

Altha is unable to make out why she's dreaming this way, but it is preventing her from accepting the transformation sequence; despite being in hyper sleep.

'Unum's heartbeat has been elevated the last four days,' Altha makes a note in her chart and sends it directly to the master system.

***

CHAPTER 14

I look at the reflection in the glass window and feel the wound inflicted on me that's finally healing; since Altha has awoken me from my sleep.

A pink scar on my nose and cheek are the only visible gifts the nightspects left for me. A friendly reminder to stay away from areas I don't have permission to venture into.

At my station, I look at Ziv and her slightly pinkish skin, I shudder to think of sleeping in a box for ten years. I guess I should really be thankful I haven't had an anal probe, I chuckle to myself. I have a sick sense of humor.

Pushing the thoughts out of my mind I begin the daily log in and start the task of endless questions about earth as I am to answer this machine, this is my job here.

Hour's pass, and I am developing a new headache.

I rub my forehead and try to concentrate, zoning out.

Ziv taps me on the shoulder and is standing beside me, I didn't even see her walk over.

"Take this, don't show Torga. It should help with the headaches," she whispers in my ear.

I look over at Ziv who holds the yellow pill in her hand. "Ziv, I am not going to take your weird alien medicine but thank you."

"Listen, I don't have time to explain it right now, just take it. You'll thank me later."

Ziv walks back to her station just before Torga notices that she left. He looks at us both and resumes his work.

I look at the pill once more, careful to conceal it and make it appear as though I am looking at my screen. It glistens in the artificial light. There appears to be a number on it, one.

Huh...

I again look over at Ziv, who is busily ignoring anyone and deep in her work. I take the pill dry, and it seems to easily slip down my throat a little too easy.

Within seconds my headache seems to have disappeared and my vision, now clearer. I look up and see a hue around Ziv and Torga.

'What the hell, omg, omg... okay Unum, don't freak out...' I think to myself, and I try not to panic about these new changes.

For dinner, whatever this pill did or was doing, made me violently hungry and I eat everything offered with feverish efficiency.

I look around and I see the vastness of hues in different strengths of vibrant fuchsia pinks, and all the other colors around some of the others.

'Why is everyone glowing?' I say out loud as I curiously I look down at my arms and see nothing out of the ordinary, except for the fact I can now see my veins, blood, and bone through my skin.

"Holy shit!"

Ziv grabs me by the arm, and quickly I am forced to sit down with her, far off from the others.

"Quiet, they will all hear you. Everyone here is heightened in senses since leaving incubation. Listen, that pill I gave you was from one of the oldest and most original formulas left on this planet. She's dying, our ruler. But unlike her, who seems to remember things and make things that we don't understand, that pill is from long ago. Torga had this in his room. No one is able to create such things, which means there must have been a time when we were not ruled by the likes of her. And after studying that pill in secret it over the last six months, I discovered its bizarre unique properties, so I stole the rest of them."

"Okay? I'm not following."

Ziv sighed in exasperation.

"Ugh, Humans. Torga knows that these pills are special. That's why he hides them in his room. And I think that you know that those pills will be able to help you. Don't you want to go home?"

"What? Help me? Are you serious? Of course, I want to go home, but..."

Ziv looked around the room, and for the first time I saw the human sadness surface briefly in her eyes then shift back to that blank expression.

Ziv interrupted, "It's too late for me now. But it isn't for you. She told me that they have been trying to get you to transition that it hasn't been working. Your body rejects all the different techniques that the Imagorna has perfected for everyone but you. You must leave this place and follow the path to get to her. But do not go off the path, otherwise it can cause significant destruction of the planet's precious resources. I am not sure of the connection; our planet becomes volatile. You must find a way to get us out of here. Everyone else here is contaminated with the planet, but you."

"Ziv, I tried to see how to get out of here before and ended up with a head trauma, so, I don't much feel like facing the nightsects again."

"In a few days, I will arrange for an opportunity to give you a chance to leave here, but you must prepare as there is no food for you to eat or anyway to sustain a human in that atmosphere. But that pill will start to help you to be able to breathe when you go outside of here, according to my calculations. My hopes are that it will also suppress your hunger, or at least delay it for a while. I took great care to get it to you, I will die if Torga discovers it was me that took it. I will give you one pill a day, for the next few days, until my supply runs out. I believe you will need to take before you will be to roam freely out there, it doesn't hurt you, it just helps you be able to breathe the atmosphere."

I shift uncomfortably in my chair.

"That and x-ray vision...Why now, why are you helping me? Are you coming with me? I can't do this alone. More importantly, how do you know those pills aren't part of this planet?"

"I have come to be attached to you Unum; I have listened to all your stories about your life. I believe it to be you that will free us all from this place, this prison. I don't want to become fully, one of them. I would much rather die then turn into them, it's bad enough now. I have changed, and there is nothing I can do. For once in your life, you need to trust someone, I mean you no harm. The pill is not from the flower compound, I have tested it in secret. She has eyes, but I, have my own methods."

"Don't you get to live forever? It can't be all that bad being one of them."

Ziv waited as an Imagornian walked by before she spoke.

"Do you have any idea how painful it is to go through the transformation? You cannot scream out in agony, only inside your head. Until it makes you feel insane! Ten years of day-in-day-out pain, as the gasses seep into my pores and into my veins to change my DNA and everything that made me human. I have lost so much already. I cannot feel as much as I once did. I feel numb, and I feel something is inside of me; like I am just a host for an alien that is living in my body. It crawls around within the confines of my skin. This is no way to live."

"Oh Ziv... I don't know what to say." I reached out and touched her arm, it vibrates.

"You must stop this; Unum, you are one of many, but you are the *only* human that can save, us. We are not a perfected race turning into them, and what they would want us to be, hosts. I am not human anymore; they have killed me slowly. No, 'Her' she has done this to me, to everyone, I just can't prove it." Ziv looked into my eyes as she spoke.

I knew what I had to do.

***

CHAPTER 15

"Hey kiddo, Are you still having fun selling those flowers for us? Have I got a job for you, how about you babysit my kids the week of Mother's Day instead of selling? I'll make it worth your while!"

"Thanks Chris, but I think I would make more money by selling flowers instead." I adjusted my shirt. He always made me feel uncomfortable and I didn't know why. Maybe it was just because I didn't trust males in general, or the fact that there was something immoral about his character I couldn't quite place.

I took a job a couple months ago, before I left my mom. Jay was the driver who took us on route to sell the flowers. A bunch of us teenagers were selling them to help other kids get winter clothes, and stuff like that. Something would need soon too. It made me sell them better knowing it was to help other people, and I became one of the best sellers they had.

"I tell you what, I will give you three hundred bucks for the week if you watch my twin daughters. It's a fair deal, and you will be hanging out in my four-bedroom home with the best food and liquor a sixteen-year-old can get their hands on. I doubt you would be able to sell as much with the flowers. What do you say to that?" Chris was desperately trying to get me to accept his proposal.

He knew I was staying with Jay, and I believe he knew I had a crush on him too, which was not appropriate. Jay was twenty-six. Things were awkward, and I had nowhere else to go. I kind of liked hanging out with them though. No one put a finger on me, and Jay even gave me his room to sleep, while he slept on the couch. But I knew I couldn't stay there forever.

It was a bachelor pad with three other guys and there was never any food. Except one beer and a bottle of ketchup. The towel they used to wipe their hands, well, it could have walked away by itself, it was so disgustingly dirty.

"Okay, sure Chris I will babysit for you." It didn't take me long to decide.

The fun week of babysitting went fast, and I was out on my butt now with no place to go. I had money in my pocket but nowhere to put my two garbage bags of clothing.

I asked Jay if I could come back to stay, and he said it wasn't a good idea, especially since our boss found him and I in the same bed, sleeping in on a lazy Sunday morning. Something I had provoked because he was tipsy and late to come home to sleep, plus there was a new person crashing on the couch.

I was homeless.

I asked Chris if he wouldn't mind storing my stuff for a brief time, he said it was ok and also said I could sleep on the school bus until I figured things out.

That evening I went to the bar because I looked older than I was at sixteen and I needed to forget my problems. I met this guy at a bar, he offered me a job, selling driveway sealing packages to people. It sounded like something similar to what I had already done, selling stuff, and I was good at it, so I accepted.

I tried a beer for the first time and didn't care for the taste, the bartender pulled me aside and told me he knew I wasn't old enough to be in here. He told me to finish the drink with my new friends, but he didn't want to see my face in here again. I thanked him for not kicking me out. I wouldn't go back there again.

I was, however, way too trusting, and I also ac-

accepted this guy's coach, which was a better offer than the school bus.

I slept as well as I could that night, being in a strange old guy's house.

When I got up, he told me to help myself to whatever I wanted, just please make him a coffee. His girlfriend heard and told him to fuck off and argued that was her job. I didn't even know she was there, the new voice startled me.

"Hey, I am Cherry, I am the old lady of the house. Don't listen to him, eh, you listen to me. You don't have to do anything. Just work for him, make us some money and we're square." She took a draw from her cigarette and put her fingers through her tangled hair.

Cherry, was a bleach blonde, seemed kind of rough around the edges by her demeanor, she had a lot of tattoos, but she seemed nice.

Shortly after she left, I made a coffee and sat down on the couch, careful not to touch anything.

Mark sat down beside me.

"So, you like it here? you comfortable?"

“Yes, thank you. I appreciate you letting me stay here. I will do my best to sell and make money.” I suddenly felt nervous.

“Don’t listen to that bitch, whatever she tells you, she’s a crack head, she just uses me for drugs. But you are young and beautiful. Has anyone ever told you how pretty you are? You do things for me here, and I will give you whatever you want. You understand what I am saying?” He leaned in and planted his wrinkled dry, fifty-year-old lips on me.

I froze. I needed to get out of here.

I stood up, “ I must go now, a panic filled my throat. I need to see where my clothes are.”

“Hey now, don’t be scared, I’m not going to hurt you. Come here and sit next to me.”

“No, I really must go, otherwise my ex-boss might throw out my stuff and I won’t have anything to wear.

Please, I must go right now." My heart was beating out of my chest and beads of sweat trickled down my face.

"Okay, just make sure you don't come back too late. I want a decision about *my offer,* I think it's the best offer you will get, as you have no place to go. Besides, I can buy you new clothes, better clothes. Sexy ones." He winked at me.

I nodded backing up toward the door, nearly throwing up my coffee.

In a flash, I left, I didn't even take the elevator. It was on the sixth floor, and I don't even recall how I got outside the building, not until the fresh falling air hit my face.

Tears staining my face I realized I was still homeless, now jobless, and didn't have any of my possessions. I wish I could just go home. But I was not going back to mom.

I ran across the street to another small plaza, still viewing the apartment building I just ran out of and sat by the curb.

A man pulled up in his white sports car. I didn't know him, but he looked harmless, but then again so did that creepy old man I just ran from.

"Hey, are you okay?" he called to me as he unrolled the passenger side window.

"No, I am not okay. Please leave me alone." I tucked my head in between my legs and hid my face.

He shut his car off, got out of the car and stood to face me.

"I am not leaving until I see a smile on that face. What's a pretty girl like you doing in a parking lot crying?

Please, let me help you. There is anything I can do?"

"I just got hit on by an old man and he kissed me, I have my clothes somewhere on a school bus I can't locate, and I am currently homeless. I doubt you can help me." I wiped a tear on my sleeve.

"How about I give you a ride to get your clothes then. Then we can figure out the next steps, okay? I swear to my daughter's life, I will not touch you. Let me just help you. My daughters are about your age. How old are you?"

"I'm sixteen."

"My name's Tim, do you know where your clothes are? I don't have any plans right now, so let's go get them."

"Okay, but please don't try anything funny, I will scream, and everyone will hear, I'm Unum."

"No problem, Unum. I'll scream too if anyone touches me."

"What?" I laughed.

"Ha! I see a smile! Let's go."

***

CHAPTER 16

The analogous transformation of saturated thermorganictech into the third-generation alien species, are in fact, quite beautiful.

Their skin is smooth, and the grooved lines streamlined their faces, perfecting their strength and agility. The large glowing, circular neon pink rings for eyes, heightened thermal sight. It enhanced it to see clearly in the dark, which is needed out in space.

Their heart shaped lips and angled nose do not give the appearance of something fierce; but rather it has the presence of peace.

Their slender bodies with natural hover abilities are vastly different than the initial human structure. The utilitarian function of stationary legs that were used to push muscles to walk, is not needed, but used to mimic the same function of movement.

The gaseototech is also made from the structure of the vast white cathedral, which has a protective coating to prevent plant life from seeping inside. It also acts like a natural barrier to the native animals. This prevents them from coming within several meters of the building.

Some gamma ray lasers, when hit with Pico technology are mixed with the alien plant byproduct, that go into sealed tubular structures, heated at high temperatures creating a liquid atomically accelerated alien fabric. This is used to create drones and other hard surface materials needed to withstand the light speeds of space.

The design is presented in such a way to prevent permanent damage to its walls. It was created with nuclear isomers bonding to the gases of the alien roseus which if damaged, can regenerate itself.

The Imagorna welds long fabricated strips of the cooled material in alignment and are put together meticulously by the second-generation staff.

The cathedral, when it's time, and once it is fully constructed, will become a ship vessel that will launch them off the planet.

Right now, it is deeply rooted embedded and bonded to the planet and cannot launch until the right amount of matter has been absorbed.

The nightspect's have had no need to patrol the outer perimeter of the area. There was no violence among the species up to this point, and it has remained this way for generations.

Lately, there have been small earthquakes. The last one which had caused hairline cracks on the cathedral shaped ship, is repairable through, over time, due to the fact that it is a living organism.

Torga's work, a seemingly daunting job, is to inform the master- 'she,' regarding all matters. Those who wear these organic eyes will send off of any unusual anomalies and this gets directed into a mainframe, much like a computer where all the information is stored. This was unheard of with the third transformation species.

The remaining humans are finalizing, currently only a handful remain. They will be devoid of emotion, a flawless perfected version of a human.

The eyes on the garments are the eye of the flower's center, taken and carefully removed of their gentle delicate petals. They are inserted with part of the stem still intact, they being called, living garments. These connect to 'her' and are encased in a metallic telepathic material which was specially created to keep track of everyone on the planet. The petals act as a rich vitamin and food protein used to create the sustenance needed to feed the planet.

Any major changes in anomaly of both plants, alien, and human, will be recognized as a threat and will send an automated message of urgency.

The day the quake cracked the walls was the same time that one of the newest third gens had an emotional moment of sheer anger. Unheard of.

The Imagorna consider this to be a sickness. The first of their kind. Isolating it to study the origins of the infection by confining it to hyper sleep. By doing this it is slowing the process of the entity itself for whatever is causing its degeneration.

Altha is the head of the department and is to lead in the process of any new discovery. This station is located near the mouth of the city.

The replacement is Ethymena, a younger but fast learner to watch over and study where Unum was currently residing.

***

CHAPTER 17

I took the fourth pill given to me last night, right before bed. Pretending to cough so the eyes on my outfit hanging in the far end of my pod, cannot see me take it.

I was told to be ready as soon as I leave my room in the morning, like clockwork. Nothing could appear different. Something or someone would signal me. It was vague, and I wasn't sure how much I could really trust Ziv, but I really didn't have a choice.

I needed to get off this planet.

Tonight, I had trouble sleeping. I was way too nervous about leaving this place, it had become my safe haven, ironically. I had no idea what to expect out there. I haven't set foot outside since I've been here.

I don't even remember how I got here.

Just that I woke up in this dome and that's how my life has been ever since.

My dreams have been really intense since I got here. Every night, I dream of a moment of my youth. I am older, and I really thought I had made peace with my past. Yet here I am, dreaming about it like it's an unresolved matter. Maybe all that therapy really was a waste like I thought, and I didn't resolve any of my issues.

All I knew was that it was eating away at me

thoughts. It makes me feel like I am re-living my youth, every night. The emotions are so strong, and it pulls at me. I wake in a pool of my own sweat and in the morning I feel as though I didn't sleep at all, I am constantly tired.

Hours later, I look out and I can see beyond the horizon, as the light cascades off my glass ceiling; I can't believe I have been awake all night. *Overthinking again.*

The alarm goes off and I pretend to drop the book as I always do. Keeping the routine all the same, as much as I can.

The dome begins to smoke over as usual, so I can change.

I take deep breaths; I tell myself I am ready. But inside, I am terrified, I can feel the anxiety creeping up to welcome me with my heart beating out of my chest. I've got to calm down, I start counting my breaths. I am not changing into my day clothes. Those eyes are not coming with me.

The door evaporates, and standing on the other side, is a single guard. I freeze in place.

The nightspect says nothing to me and grabs my arm. It hurriedly takes me down the tunnels in the opposite direction of my station. My mind is racing,' do they know that I was planning to leave? How? Where is it taking me?' I started to fight it, but the grip was too strong.

It never looks at me at all, we come upon a silver door that is raining on itself. It's chrome-like material, it reminds me of the table I saw in the medical room I was in.

The nightspect starts to push a series of buttons with symbols I cannot read.

The door slides open, and it pushes me violently outside and immediately the door starts closing quickly behind me. In a fraction of a second, before it seals shut; I see Ziv take off her mask to reveal herself to me.

"What?... How?...Ziv!"

I suddenly realize, I am free, and she is gone behind that door.

I am also out in the open and exposed, here for anyone else who might be watching to see.

I sprint for cover.

CHAPTER 18

Altha receives a message from Ethymena. It blinks and flashes on her screen:

'Unum is not sleeping. What is the protocol for this?'

Altha has not come across this before, but knowing that Unum sustained a head trauma, there could be residual complications.

RESPONSE: 'Monitor it.'

Ethymena does as she is instructed with no new prompts from Unum.

All night, I remain awake. My heart rate elevates. Something is scaring me. The unknown, I don't know if I can do this. My head is spinning.

Ethymena, *notes; scared emotion, no dreams.* Yet the same reaction while awake.

She makes notes and inputs it for her report.

Altha continues to do her work. She has isolated the virus with the samples of tissue she had taken.

She sees the flaws of the third-generation humanoid. It has an insignificant reversal DNA altercation in his transformation. Which seems impossible.

The mechanics have been flawless with respect to the gas ratio and age secretion infiltration timelines. How is this possible...

Altha continues to investigate and makes a report to 'her, Alzar.'

***

CHAPTER 19

Miles from the spaceship site, the lack of light is slowly beginning to kill the plants. Slowly the pink beautiful roseus flowers are beginning to turn into a blackened dust. The pathway to where 'she,' Alzar resides, is dark.

Her, a once beautiful gown of pastel pinks she wears, is fading and seeping into black and grey.

"I am dying," she says in a low tone.

I can feel myself still connected to the planet but the conversion to separate is taking far too long.

I stand emotionless at the gateway into my once beautiful garden. I stand still, like a porcelain doll. Hollow and hauntingly pale with intense eyes, I look nothing like those beautiful aliens.

I am pale with a human face, a form I took on many years ago as I grew here. My eyes are black. My arms are like roots and protrude out five endings, replicating hands.

I sense my time is drawing near, everything that is connecting to me, pulling me in and withdrawing my powers. I looking off into the distance, I see it has already taken over, the only home I chose that resides on this planet, the only pathway that leads to me, all dying.

My eyes glow pink as I try to signal for help through telekinesis, to any living thing passing by out of orbit and beyond, who may catch it. To any of the others like me who might still be out there, floating. The only strength I have left is to do this one thing, signaling. Once a day it drains my energy completely. Who knows how many ships have passed and were uninformed I needed help.

There is no way off this living hell of a home, now we are all going to die.

The transformation of humans to immortal alien species was the chance to separate me from the planet. To put the living organisms into the humans and take them away from this place so that a piece of the planet would remain inside them, a piece of me.

Keeping them as fresh resources for future placement and nutrients, the thermorganictech pico-tech modules in their purest form to be stored, protected, and living in them was a brilliant idea, to move them to other planets to infect other species, breathing new spores to everything and everyone when the time was right.

It would have worked to if it wasn't for Unum's encephalon, something we just can't fix.

Converting the planet matter into a living energy that never dies would mean the planet would live on in a separate way, I would live on.

I could dance amongst the stars, just as before.

It was essential Unum be part of it and with the dwindling plants, there was no way to fuel the drones so that I could get more humans from earth to fill the void.

I couldn't sacrifice any more of my precious planet resource, my children, me. All that I had done to convert the humans, and I am failing.

INCOMING MESSAGE forms a liquid translucent screen in front of my face: 'Discovery. Third Gen flaw. DNA anomaly.'

INCOMING MESSAGE: 'Unum, sleepless. Scared emotion during night of wakefulness. Elevated heart rate.'

INCOMING MESSAGE: Unum has escaped.

***

CHAPTER 20

I run until my legs hurt. This is the first time I've felt alive here on this planet. My heart is beating fast with terror and excitement. To be able to use these muscles again at full capacity, feels like a dream.

I follow the path which seems to naturally form from the way is worn, a smooth flat rock formation in slabs of what looks like granite like the walls, are here too.

A bright marbleized pink with flecks of iridescent colors is almost pulsing underneath my feet. *Glowing with life.*

I gaze upward at the evolved planet with awe.

High above it looks as though the planets are reflecting in a glass window. The spectacle of fuchsia pink plants with trails of filament are moving gently in the warm wind as if it were waving me over, beckoning me to follow.

It felt dream like to be here, the sky filled with pink and the bright galaxy stars, as far as the eye could see. The planet above looks more like a pink sun than a planet. Perhaps it was, I thought. Not really knowing what to make of my surroundings as I continued to walk deeper into the wild alien landscape as it swallows me from the celestial tower's view.

The darkness doesn't come, even after hours go by. That pink light in the sky never fading off or changing position, no matter how far I have walked. The light I cannot look upon anymore, my eyes have become tired. I am feeling hungry too, but I don't know what to eat or drink.

'It's not safe,' I have to remind myself, even as I come upon something of what looks to be like bush of berries. An unusual color as it shines a purple-blue-yellow metallic, depending, on the angle you look at it.

The shape is deceiving, reminding me of strawberries and my mouth begins to water at the sight of potential food.

I continue despite my protesting tummy angrily growling and asking for sustenance.

I see off in the distance it has become quite dark, less color radiating from the flowers now. Oddly, I turn around to justify what I am seeing. So, it is getting darker the further I walk on.

I continue to walk for many miles and my tired muscles cry out and demand that I stop. I look around and listen in silence for any incoming nightspects. All but the gentle rustling of the plantation, is what I hear.

Off the trail, is a clearing and it looks so inviting to take a nap in. The surrounding area is a protection for me, and I think will be unseen there.

My foot takes a gentle step off the trail and on to the untouched land. I step on it with my other foot, stop and wait for something to happen. *Nothing happens.*

The ground feels warm beneath my feet, and it radiates through the soles of my shoes and onto my skin, as it moves up my legs and around my thighs. It tingles, I curiously look at my hands and even now, my whole body vibrates gently.

I am used to seeing my veins and bones when I

look at my hands, a product of the pill. I don't feel any different I can breathe out here.

It doesn't feel like it's a danger, so I continue to walk to a clearing, careful not to disturb the vegetation and especially since there are so much less of the precious flowers here.

Sitting in the small clearing amongst the taller plants, it does seem to provide me with a place to hide. I feel that I am safe from the nightspects. Sleep is calling me; I cannot fight it any longer. I toss and turn until I find the fetal position and quickly drift off to sleep.

The eyes are watching.

CHAPTER 21

A thunderous eruption from a tremor creates new hairline cracks in the building.

Torga pushes buttons and frantically tries to stabilize it. With the newly installed sway bars put in place that have come down from the ceiling to the floor, reinforces the structure to help brace for impact.

Ziv and Torga hold on to the table as it shakes violently.

"Shouldn't we be abandoning the system and seek refuge to somewhere safer?"

"This is the safest place to be Ziv, this place was built to withstand the emergency contingencies of a worst-case scenario. I can't imagine it lasting much longer than last time."

Ziv didn't speak but thought of Unum, and realized she didn't mention again the importance of staying on the path. It must be her doing this, without even realizing it.

Torga sends an urgent message to Alzar.

'INCOMING MESSAGE: URGENT; Quakes are substantial. Connection to escaped human. Please advise.'

Torga being the oldest on the planet, was one of the only ones who called the leader by her name. He never uttered it to others, as it seemed to be against some unwritten policy or law to speak of it.

He, being the eldest, saw the celestial building being built, he was one of the ones to bind the materials together many moons ago. He even went on expeditions to other planets before everything changed. When they used to be free.

He built and designed and engineered countless tech for their planet, right down to the glass domes which housed the humans, and alien species.

Ziv looked at Torga side eyed and tried not to give away anything she was thinking.

"Ziv, I need you to go to the medical department and see if there are any updates on that patient being held there."

"But Torga, you need me here; I don't want to leave you."

"I can't seem to be able to send any messages due to the substantial damage we are sustaining. The longer this keeps up, the worse it will be. The third-generation pods are starting to fail, and lives are going to be lost if we can't figure this out quickly. I need to stay here and watch the..." A huge chunk of the wall crushes onto Togra. Ziv falls under the violent shakes and debris and becomes buried underneath the rubble.

The rumbling continues to break the walls and crack the building further, faster than the regenerative repair can handle.

Altha is desperately trying to send a message to Torga and Ethymena, but their signals are jammed. The lines that control the integration of gases have been stunted and cut out. Damaged by the quakes.

Altha is looking at the translucent screen as it blinks red, the pods have stopped working. She looks up and sees him, standing there in a daze. She grabs for anything to use but it's too late, the enraged a reawakened patient who was in hyper sleep, now takes the shards of opulent alien glass and stabs her with vicious malicious intent. Plunging the shard into the side of her neck.

Altha grabs hold of her neck and falls to the floor gagging on the neon purple fluid draining out of her.

The patient who is standing over her grips the shard tighter. Attacking again and this time it doesn't stop until those pink rings for eyes grow dark.

He then takes the shard dripping with Altha's blood, and impales himself, he falls to the floor, dead.

It is hours before Altha opens her eyes once regenerated and proceeds to dispose of the defective human.

This attack means an infection is spreading.

CHAPTER 22

I don't want to get up, it's been so long since I have slept so well. I feel as though I am in a trance. I stretch out and put my hands under my head and look up at the sky. It's so clear you can see thousands of stars, even in the light of the day beyond the fluffy nebula-like clouds. It is spectacular.

I am so tired that sleep captures me yet again, and I drift in and out of slumber again and again, for the next few hours. I vaguely remember I shouldn't be here, touching the ground. I am too tired to care.

I dream only of my cat, Bumkin. At first it is a happy memory, and then it changes; the tears start to escape from my eyes. I am on the phone, and my mom has just told me she put my precious boy to sleep because he stopped eating after I left.

“You should have come for him; you should never have never left him; he was your cat after all no one to blame but you…” her voice echoing in the walls of my mind…she killed him because of me.

A nearby crunch snaps me awake; I am now nose-to-nose with a creature that’s drooling hot liquid on my face. As it drips on my skin, it feels like it is burning me. It is as hot as standing too close to a fire. It's so bad, that I jump up, scream, and grab my face. The creature is the size of an adult raccoon, and it shows me its teeth. Hundreds if not thousands of tiny sharp daggers protrude from its mouth and its large eyes that never seem to blink as it slowly positions itself between me and the path.

Its fur is matted, a bright blue with spikes in random places on its body. It only has two legs, and it looks cute enough to pet, yet its creepy face sets me into panic mode.

I back up into a stump of alien matter and am looking for possible ways out of this situation. My knees get wobbly as I see yet another creature appearing in view; this one is unlike the blue one. Its pink fur matches the flowers and has equally sharp teeth and a large mouth.

Gracefully, but bravely, I delicately take a step to the side and see what kind of reaction it will incur in these beasts.

Both open their mouths and let out a horrific noise. It compares to the sound of a thousand fingernails on a chalk board. I freeze and hold my hands up to my ears as I am pretty sure this will make me deaf. I can almost feel that my ears must be bleeding.

I believe this is the end for me now, and I lean as far as I can against the overgrowth, I am trapped. I guess this is how it ends.

***

CHAPTER 23

The nightspect's are now deployed out onto the field, they are careful not to step off the path. They hover over it, never touching the surface. I had this protection layer put in place, so that whatever happens they would surround me until my last breath and be there to govern over me while I die. They will die too, but they know not of their fate.

The remains of the house and that of the owner, have grown dark. The once vibrant plant life that was Intertwined like thick layers of tangled yarn, is now incased with it, within this dense area. The eyes that were on my gown look more like a series of veins that appear to have spread all over my body to cover me. All eyes are now a dull, the force of life growing weaker by the minute. The beautiful pink planet is dying and at its core, and I Alzar, will be the first to go.

I look upon my fingers turning grey and blackened at the tips, I but a flower myself, a frail moment of time. The cycle of life I have avoided for thousands of years.

Looking upon the skies tries one last time to signal again.

My heart is failing, all three of them. One is connected to the planet, the other, the plantation.

The tears that fall from my face slowly slide and cascade down, rolling from her cheeks creating deep burns and spilling onto her dress, changing its color from pale pink to completely black.

***

CHAPTER 24 

I brace for impact, but something about them seems to change. It's as though they are listening to something I cannot hear. They salivate, but whatever is coming is far worse as they cock their heads to the side and become frozen.

A cold breeze whips by them and the creatures lay flat to the ground as if terrified and bracing for impact themselves.

An elongated pale metallic pink ship with a disc-like front that spins, hoovers over us. The size of the ship, large enough to hold a small city. It was unlike anything I had ever seen.

The wind generated from it is picking up and blowing the vegetation and me, I am struggling to keep standing.

I look up and see a bright light highlighting me and the surrounding area, including the creatures.

How is this possible? They told me they can't fly out of here. I think to myself.

The creatures are slowly inching and backing away, never looking at me or the ship.

I watch them leave, the noise of the wind that the ship creates is howling in my ears. I looked up into the light and began to rise off the ground. I frantically try to grab on to the vegetation, but it slips and breaks from my hands as I continue to be propelled upwards toward the ship.

As if dissolved, I reappear in liquid form at first, and I am translucent, and although I am screaming, no one can hear, not even me. I am now standing inside of the ship.

I fall to my knees and look at my hands. I touch my body and briefly to check it over. It's all there but, is it really me or some replica of me?

“What the fuck...”

Altha is standing over me.

“I fear humans do not appreciate our technology. I am here to take you to Alzar. 'She,' is dying. You know not of what you have just done to our planet, Unum. How one earthling could have this much impact? We are all going to die.”

The muscle in my jaw flexes. Silence falls suddenly on the ships mates as I stare at Altha.

“Listen to me, I never asked to be here. I never asked to be placed from my home to this god forsaken planet. I just wanted to go home. I don’t give a shit about what is happening to your planet. Take me back home! We are all going to die. Well, you know what, that would be a more blessing than being trapped here."

"Be that as it may Unum, you may not care, but you will. All the lives on the planet are hanging in the balance because of you. I don't blame you for your confusion but when you see everyone dead, mad from the poison of the planet that consumes them, you will."

I find myself squeezing my knuckles till they turn white; my nails dig into my skin until it breaks through. I can feel my blood trickle out. My anger boils over me as I want to strike everyone and everything.

"I do not understand," I spat out through my teeth.

"The planet is feeding and keeping everything alive."

"Soon, after the last parts of the connected stems of this planet die off, you will too. Once everything dies it will not sustain life, it will be poisonous, and it will float out among space a dead planet, killing everything and anything in its path, stars, species, and earth."

"You are talking another language to me; I do not understand..." I am unconsciously rubbing my forehead. I have a migraine.

Altha puts her hand on my arm to silence me.

"All will be revealed, Unum. We have been here for over a hundred thousand earth years. We want to be free of this place, just as you do."

Altha turned and spoke to one another, and they took then me by either arm escorted me to my new chambers.

I sit on the hovering bed and looked out at the pink blur whipping by through the window and began to think. *'If they only knew how much I have been through, how much I hated my planet for what my parents put me through... but even though I am angry, there must be more to life than this. I am a spec in the vastness of life. I am insignificant. My parents told me this all my life, and at first I was glad I wasn't on earth anymore. Everyone in my life has shown me just how much they didn't want me around. Now I am here, on this pink planet, and I am important? No. They will see I am just as ordinary as anything. I have no influence on the lives of this planet, just like on earth.'*

***

CHAPTER 25

The luminescent neon pink streaks the sky, like the nights on earth, those days when I would catch the northern lights.

It's a beautiful planet but time is up.

The Imagorna species are dying. They are reborn but once every hundred years. It keeps the population steady but not overpopulated, unlike earth.

The cycle of their lives was ageless.

They go through a phase, a time to hibernate, shed old skin, and the cell replacements improve themselves and rejuvenate.

They are wiser for every transformation phase for they are also given uploads and vital information for future survival. The ones left by those before them, a gift of knowledge.

Since the change on the planet and she has taken over them, the species are not able do this essential need, which is causes them to die.

Humans were brought to absorb and transcend the old ways, to appease the planet.

To shift nature's codes with biomodifications. It should have worked. Alzar had calculated the percentile, and it was at ninety three percent success rate, which is why she chose to habitat it with her life force, the alien plant life to help them become better, become her.

Alzar was a tiny alien spore wandering in space, saw the pink planet and decided to attach herself to it and breed.

The plants, her babies, feed the planet, the species, and the humans.

The food for the Imorgana was sustainable. The cycle of the planet was a perfect breeding ground.

Alzars invisible roots entangled all life and purpose here. No singular life was individualized onto another.

One spore is but a piece of something bigger. Alzar altered the balance of life here and ruined it.

The pink from the plant's flickers into space like car headlights pointing toward the heavens, giving off her toxic glowing pink rays. Her children gently dance in the sway of the breeze from the gases it omits, more future spores to send out into space.

***

CHAPTER 26

The pink sun never moves off in the distance, as it touches the glass window that brightens my chambers in the spaceship. I am glad to have a window to look out, it seems as though we are just orbiting around the planet.

The warmth of the sun hits my face, as I begin to remember the nightmare and reality of what's happening, and I sit up violently and look around. 'Still here,... and I keep telling myself this is just a dream, a beautiful nightmare.' I mutter to myself.

I get dressed and am greeted by Altha who has impeccable timing, "I trust you slept well. Your vitals showed no signs of nightmares last night. This is the first change we have seen since you arrived. How do you feel?"

"Jeez, you know everything don't you, ever heard of a little thing called privacy? If you must know, I don't remember dreaming last night, no."

“Good. Now we must proceed with an injection to evaluate my theory. I want to see if you are now ready to receive the planet’s organic materials to start your transition. We don’t have time to do the usual ten-year process. We will need to speed it up in a new hyperactive chamber we’ve created especially for you.” Altha started scanning me where she stood.

“Um, let me think about it for a second. NO! I am not putting crap into my body to save your planet you all can just die for all I care. "I left the room and proceeded to run to the deck of the ship.

Altha nodded to the other two guards, and they squirted the needle to let the remaining air out before following me.

I looked at the others running the ship as I pushed one aside and began pushing all the buttons and moved some levers upward which accelerated the ship to propel it upwards and away from the planet.

“I want off of this planet!” I screamed, my anger was visible, and the others backed away.

"Unum, we want the same thing. Just take the needle and help us, you are ill. We will take you home once the mission is completed. We cannot get off the planet to take you home. Our ship that came to get you is pulled back by the planet's gravitational pull. Aside from that, there are no other humans left but you to absorb the planet's essence. You are our last hope."

The ship started to shake and slammed us back and forth until it took a nosedive. We were orbiting around the planet again. A tease, we can't leave.

"No! I will not put that foreign shit in my body, you can just fuck off, because I will kill all of you first before I let you touch me!" I backed up into one of the guards.

In an instant the needle was inserted into my neck, and I fell to the floor, everything grew dark.

CHAPTER 27

'It's been 30 days since the first injection. Unum's vital signs are stable but rejecting it. Her heartbeat is elevated, and she is hallucinating. She believes I am her mother and is not cooperating with every cell of her body. She does not go into a sleep state. I have never seen anything like it, her resistance is stronger than anything I have ever come across in a human. She was our last hope, I am afraid there is not much more I can do.'

Altha describes in detail the medical notes and sends them to Alzar.

Alzar replies, ' I would like it if you could bring her here to me.' Sent transmission.

By her bedside, a damaged but still living Ziv stares at her lifeless body, lost in her own thoughts.

Torga is dead, after being crushed by the ceiling.

It was all for nothing, as I remember being carried off staring at his lifeless body, or what's left of it. No one seems to have caught on and even if they have, care about what I've done. I've been ironically assigned to stay and monitor Unum since the tremor and the main ship needs repairs since it was forced upward. I could have helped. I should have helped. I am needed here to convince Unum to listen to reason since we are what she describes as friends.

I look at my face, the face I used to have, the skin tone... I miss my human body. The body I had has changed, morphed into a super skilled almost robotic thinking brain. I hate it. My skin is now resilient to fires and external damage caused by knives or other sharp objects. I know this because before Unum arrived, they experimented on me.

Now she's here, she is supposed to be our way out. I can feel it to my core. Something about her, she's the one who will save us. As I see her in this state, so fragile, so pale, I wonder if we were wrong.

***

I have been in the bed for hours stirring from the nightmares that have returned to me. I can't open my eyes, but I feel as though there is a battle going on inside my body.

Ziv communicates with Altha directly and gives updates on my progress.

I can hear whispers from a familiar voice. I stir in the bed.

“Unum? You are required to wake up.” Ziv leans in to check her vitals.

CHAPTER 28

Alzar is standing by the doorway of the black decrepit house that was once prestigious and royal, to let us into her home. Alzar refused to get on the ship despite the growing blackness.

"Bring her inside and lay her on the table I have provided for her," stepping aside to let the nightspect's in that are carrying her body.

Ziv bows as they all do when they see her, "Alzar oh master of this planet, what can she do in order to save us all?"

"That I do not know, I cannot foresee this future timeline like the others. But I know we must awaken her." Alzar begins touching Unum's forehead with her blackened long pointy fingers.

I feel as though my body is made of lead, its heavy and not responding to my cries as I briefly look upon Alzars, face. I want to rip my eyes from my skull as her face resembles that of my mother's. I feel myself slowly losing my sanity and every second that inches by I am failing to grasp reality and fiction.

"Welcome Unum, I have used my dying powers to

awaken you, the tube that's injected into your veins is directly connected to me. Even as I stand here, my life force is being drawn out. Soon, I will be dead, as will the planet unless I can get myself into you."

I sit up and look down at my arm, I am screaming. I hear my voice now which sounds foreign to me.

"GET THE FUCK OUT OF ME!" Without thinking I grab her vines that are now under my skin and trying to envelope me. I rip it from my body and despite the pain I cannot feel it from the adrenaline, as I wrap it around her neck and pull as hard as I can.

The nightspects and Ziv remain frozen in place, it's only Altha only who is trying to pry me free from her.

But I have superhuman strength, push her aside with my free hand. I will not let Alzar go, until her last breath exits.

CHAPTER 29

The planet shakes as it begins to crack down its center, the plants and life fall through into the darkness of abyss. The black hole filling out and deep into the ground. Ripped and torn into chunks pieces of the planet breaks off and slowly descends into space.

We are all going to die.

Even though my body had finally taken on some of the planet's organic matter, it is still not enough to stop it.

I *killed* Alzar. I know she is the enemy.

I see her thoughts and what she's done and now there is nothing left to stop this planet from disintegrating.

Ziv and Altha were wrong about me, I cannot save them, I cannot even save myself from my mind. Those nightmares that have haunted me every night and every day of my waking life.

I run out of Alzar's house, the chunks fly by me as the planet's atmosphere is broken and torn apart, I look upon the vastness of the planet's beauty, gone.

The planet shifts violently, and I am thrown violently to the crumbling ground beneath me like dust, the pink lined horizon is no more than a memory, only blackness fills the skyline, and the decay of vegetation is seen all over what's left of the planet's surface.

I look down at the growing space between ground and the planet's core, it opens up wide to swallow me whole. Nothing left here, I can't leave, I'm infected,... so I jump into the abyss.

My hair lifts off my face and I feel weightless. The world becomes silent as I dive into the planet's core. Everything slows, as I feel the speed of the drop erupting my eardrums.

The liquid pink of the core's planet shines out one last time and it is blinding, one final explosion, as it engulfs me in a moment, blackness.

CHAPTER 30

'Beep, beep, beep.' The monitor sparks life and my heartbeat spikes briefly on the monitor.

I stir in my bed and feel the light penetrate beneath my eyelids.

What the hell...My head is throbbing, another migraine. Am I dead?

"Welcome back, Unum. We are amazed at your recovery. We had lost hope there for a while." A doctor says this to me, and it sounds like she is far away while she checks my pulse with her cool fingertips on my skin.

"Where am I?" I rub my eyes and look at my pinkish skin. "Oh shit, no, I am not one of them, please tell me."

"There now, just relax, you will have all your abilities soon I imagine, just like the others who made it. You crashed into earth and have been in a coma for a long time.”

“What, how can that be? I was on the planet, we were trapped. I jumped off and into the planets core to die… I,… this makes no sense." I tried to sit up.

“Now, now, no getting up just yet. We really don’t know about that, but what we do know, is that you and two others were the only survivors of the crash. Whatever it is they gave you, it saved your life.” The doctor turned and left the room.

I couldn’t believe it; I was back home but now I was the alien?

I always felt different, and now I really was.

Ziv stood at the doorway with bandaged arms and a patch over one eye.

“Ziv!" I was surprised to see her my one and only friend.

"We made it home Ziv, we did it! I am so glad to see you. I thought you died. Come here and sit with me for a moment, please." I tapped my bed to invite Ziv to sit.

"Unum," she uttered as she sat on the bed beside me. "Unum don't freak out, but.. we aren't home on earth. We are still on the planet Malaxate."

"Oh, come on, they said that we are the only two survivors and those doctors were human Ziv. Have you looked outside? Help me up I want to see for myself." Tears formed in my eyes, it had to be true, I had to be home now. I could not take much more of this.

"I am sorry, I know you wanted to go home, but this is our home now and you aren't human anymore. Look at your arms. You are like me, only better. You are the new species and you saved us."

"NO Ziv, no, I am home now! I am on Earth!"

Silence.

I have to lay my head back; the room is spinning. I am too exhausted to fight this, and I fall again into a deep sleep.

"Beep, beep, beep." The monitor blinks.

Many hours later, I stir from my sleep. A hand reaches for me in the darkness.

"Are you awake my child? Please wake up. I need you to wake up and be okay. I am so sorry for everything; can you please forgive me?"

Without opening her eyes, I can still feel the headache coursing and thumping through my brain. Everything feels foggy. I attempt to open my eyes, but I cannot. I can barely move. I fight the grogginess and am able to move just one my fingers to respond to the voice.

I hear the visitor get up and scream out, 'she's awake, she's awake'... over and over.

The light shines into my eyes as the doctor examines me, lifting my eyelids. “Looks as though she’s out of the coma, your daughter is very lucky. She needs rest, not too much stimulation, so please keep her as calm as possible. I will be back in an hour to check on her again. Let me know if there are any changes.”

CHAPTER 31

Sleepily my eyes open and I can see her sitting beside me. She is older and greyer than I remember.

I must be dreaming. It's all a blur. My vision is unclear, and I can't make out where I am. I know I am in a hospital of some kind, since everything is pristine white, I don't see anything alien, yet that is. *Are this what heaven feels like?* I don't know what reality is, or if I have finally lost my mind.

Tears fall from my face, but I am alive, I know I am again somewhere else, but I didn't die. I am so scared to open my eyes. My body is shaking wildly.

"There now, I am here."

I can feel her breath on my skin, she's so close. Her hand in mine, I feel the warmth of her touch. I know who she is now, it's unmistaken.

My mother.

"Where am I?" I slowly look around to find a familiar thing or object to ground myself, but nothing looks right.

"You're in the psychiatric ward in the hospital, in

Toronto. You've been in a coma for months." All I can do is weep. I am so confused.

"So, I am on earth then?" I look at my mom and check to see if her skin and her, is human.

"Yes. You've always been on earth, hunny. I thought I lost you. You were in a coma for a year. Everything has changed since you've been here. Your dad and I aren't together anymore. I am getting help for some of my own medical problems, and I have been here every day waiting for you to come back to me." She started to cry.

"It was all a lie. Ziv and Alzar, even Torga. The abduction, all of it. I feel sick." I look at my arms to be sure I wasn't pink still, or to see where they had injected the tube. *Everything seemed human, no marks.*

"Let me go get the doctor and I will come right back, okay?" Mom sat up and started to leave.

"No, don't leave me!" I grabbed her arm.

"Okay, okay." My Mom sat back down. The doctor entered the room carrying a chart and was writing something down.

"Doctor please, I was on another planet and there were these aliens, and they were trying to get me to take this organic substance and..." I can hear the heart monitor that started to blink a warning.

"Woah, now hold on, listen sometimes when you're in a coma you can have very vivid dreams, that doesn't mean anything. It's alright you are safe. It may take some time to recover and separate the dream from reality." The doctor takes my blood pressure and looks into my eyes.

"Altha?" I vaguely recognize her, but I can hear her distinct voice. A wave of memories washes over me. "I remember you; you took care of me at first then you wanted me to become one of you!"

I push her hands back. "Stay away from me."

"Okay Unum. Mom, can we have a moment alone?

This happens sometimes in these types of cases. I am going to have a word with her and ease her mind." The doctor gently takes my mom by the arm and escorts my her to the door.

"I really think I should stay with her, she's not well enough for this..." As she looks back at me and then the doctor, the door opens, and she stands in the doorway.

"It's ok mom, not to worry. She is much stronger than you realize. I will only be a few minutes." The doctor, without waiting for a reply closes the door.

"Unum, what a unique name. Do you know its

meaning? It's Latin right?" The doctor keeps her distance.

"I know that it means one out of many. You are definitely one of the many, aren't you? Let me explain what is going on here."

I attempt to get out of bed and realize I can't move my legs; they are acting like two large heavy tree trunks. I am scared of what she is about to tell me.

"Unum. Please don't be frightened. I will explain as best I can. I am indeed, Altha. The planet was in grave danger of dying and we did bring your spirit to our planet. Your physical shell, your human body, remained here under what humans deem as a coma. We did try to injected you with the thermorganictech we made which worked on other humans, and your body initially did reject it.

But when you jumped into the planet's core you somehow absorbed it killing Alzar, all in the blink of an eye and we were freed. You see, we are all connected, you, me, this planet, and all the planets. The plants, the air we breathe, animals, everything is connected and it's the same as our planet.

Alzar, thanks to you, what you killed was an alien virus spore in our system, and yours. She had compromised our planet, and we were under her command.

Now that you have killed it and absorbed the toxins on our planet, you willed yourself to be put back to earth and into your physical body, and yet somehow have used it to healed yourself. You are an amazing piece of technological advancement. We know not of what you are capable of, or where you have come from. But, if you let me, I would like to study your abilities further." Altha smiled at me.

"My abilities aren't that great if I can't even move my legs and no more poking and studying me, I am done with that." I looked at my legs after taking the covers off.

"Will it to move and they will, it will take some effort to learn your new mechanics and figure out your abilities. You have the planet's power within you. I believe you will and can-do incredible things." Altha beamed with pride.

"I know this sounds silly, but why aren't you pink anymore, and why aren't I?" I looked at my arms like they were foreign objects.

"I believe, it is your desire to be this way, and how I look is reflected in that. Everything that happens from now on will always and has, is reflected by your desires. It can have profound consequences. Like our planet hanging in the balance due to the choices you make or made." Altha looked at her own skin and reflection in the window as she spoke.

"Okay, I sort of get it, but my mom and everything else, they have no idea about what happened right?"

"Exactly. And that should remain between us and those of us who have been there with you."

"One more thing, I killed Alzar, am I not a murderer? I had no right to do that. Wait, I am really confused. She was me? So, I was sick?"

"Yes, you only killed a part of you, the virus spore that what was inside your brain. As I said before, we are all connected. That spore created was your pain and suffering from the past, you created her, and she would have taken over you and our planet, had you not decided to overcome your past trauma. Malaxate means brain in Latin. You are a celestial being. We are all part of something much bigger. You never were just a human form on planet earth, that is only your meat suit that you choose to wear, as it were. You are and always have been a part of us, and everything, and we are part a of you. Everything is vibrational matter and what you omit out generates to planets and celestial worlds beyond. It is a huge thing to grasp I know, but you have felt this for a long time."

“Oh my god... I always have felt odd and an outcast, ever since I was a child but,... What about my parents? Where do they fit in all this?” I suddenly moved my legs, willed them, and got out of bed. Feeling empowered by the thought of being able to control my destiny as I saw fit.

I was powerful, I was someone after all.

“Your parents are in human form, yes, but they are the same as you, wearing this human meat suit also and living an earthly experience.

You chose to be placed here; well, you’re being decided it. However, it was a bad choice to leave you alone with them as you grew. But in order to grow, you needed to experience this to make you the great leader you are now. You weren’t born from your parents, but through them." Altha smiled gently.

"Oh." It took me a moment to contemplate this information. I rubbed my legs as I spoke feeling more refreshed by the minute, after I all I willed myself to be healthy.

"So, what do I do now, Altha?"

"Anything you want."

Unum.

Ziv.

Inflorescent roseus.

Torga.

Altha. 3rd Generation.

Planet Malaxate.

Alien species 1.

Alien species 2.

Author notes;

Thank you for reading this book. It has taken almost a year to research and write this book. This is my first sci-fi novel so please be gentle.

I have added my own tech and made-up new words in my world I created within this story. It is my wish to write something fresh, aside from the typical nano tech I often read in these kinds of books. I hope you enjoyed this as much as it was for me to write it.

There are Latin words within the book that may have given away a bit of the story. It is my hope that most don't know them and will be a pleasant surprise ending.

But if you caught on then I have failed you. I did try to bend your brain and leave you baffled!

Please let me know what you think and leave a review!

About the Author

Canadian Illustrator / Author Lizy J. Campbell is a self-taught artist. She is a mother of two beautiful children and works from home as an illustrator. She has many interests and currently paints pet portraits, real estate homes and more.

"I love to create. There is no limit to what I want to do, so I keep reaching for the sky. I am enthusiastic about making a difference and making people smile, one creation at a time."

www.ingramcontent.com/pod-product-compliance
Lightning Source LLC
Chambersburg PA
CBHW070400200726
48294CB00003B/1008

9781998806690